P. D. Eastman's
DOG TALES

Random House 🏠 New York

The Alphabet Book
Copyright © 1974 by P. D. Eastman, copyright renewed 2002 by Mary L. Eastman,
Peter Anthony Eastman, and Alan Eastman

Big Dog . . . Little Dog: A Bedtime Story
Copyright © 1973 by P. D. Eastman, copyright renewed 2001 by Mary L. Eastman,
Peter Anthony Eastman, and Alan Eastman

All rights reserved. Published in the United States by Random House
Children's Books, a division of Penguin Random House LLC, New York.
The stories in this collection were originally published separately in the
United States by Random House Children's Books, New York, in 1973 and 1974.

Random House and the colophon are registered trademarks
of Penguin Random House LLC.

Visit us on the Web!
rhcbooks.com

Educators and librarians, for a variety of teaching tools, visit us at
RHTeachersLibrarians.com

ISBN 978-0-593-18224-6

MANUFACTURED IN CHINA

10 9 8 7 6 5 4 3 2

Random House Children's Books supports the First Amendment
and celebrates the right to read.

Contents

P. D. Eastman

THE ALPHA

A

American ants

A
B
C
D
E
F
G
H
I
J
K
L
M
N
O
P
Q
R
S
T
U
V
W
X
Y
Z

B

Bird on bike

C

Cow in car

A
B
C
D
E
F
G
H
I
J
K
L
M
N
O
P
Q
R
S
T
U
V
W
X
Y
Z

D

Dog with drum

E

Elephant on eggs

A B C D E F G H I J K L M N O P Q R S T U V W X Y Z

A
B
C
D
E
F
G
H
I
J
K
L
M
N
O
P
Q
R
S
T
U
V
W
X
Y
Z

Fox with fish

G

Goose with guitar

A
B
C
D
E
F
G
H
I
J
K
L
M
N
O
P
Q
R
S
T
U
V
W
X
Y
Z

A
B
C
D
E
F
G
H
I
J
K
L
M
N
O
P
Q
R
S
T
U
V
W
X
Y
Z

H

Horse on house

Infant with ice cream

A
B
C
D
E
F
G
H
I
J
K
L
M
N
O
P
Q
R
S
T
U
V
W
X
Y
Z

J

Juggler with jack-o'-lanterns

K

Kangaroos with keys

A B C D E F G H I J K L M N O P Q R S T U V W X Y Z

L

Lion with lamb

M

Mouse with mask

A B C D E F G H I J K L M N O P Q R S T U V W X Y Z

N

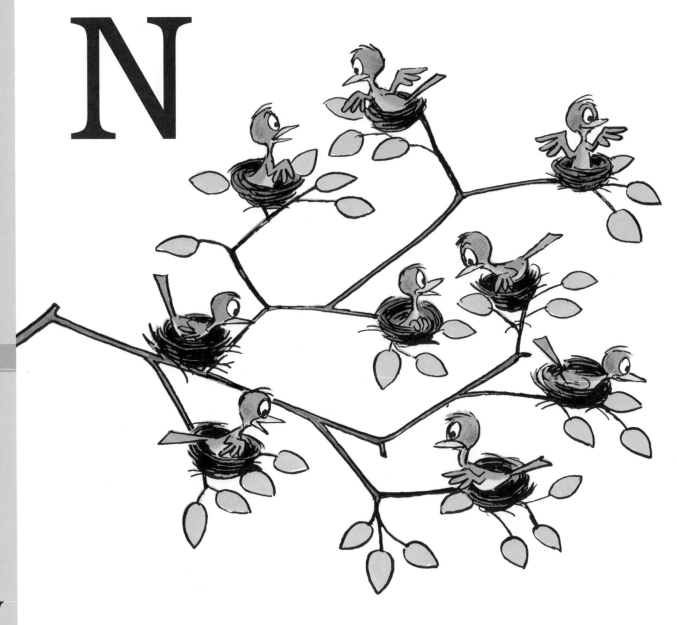

Nine in their nests

O

Octopus with oars

A
B
C
D
E
F
G
H
I
J
K
L
M
N
O
P
Q
R
S
T
U
V
W
X
Y
Z

A
B
C
D
E
F
G
H
I
J
K
L
M
N
O
P
Q
R
S
T
U
V
W
X
Y
Z

P

Penguins in parachutes

Queen with quarter

A
B
C
D
E
F
G
H
I
J
K
L
M
N
O
P
Q
R
S
T
U
V
W
X
Y
Z

A
B
C
D
E
F
G
H
I
J
K
L
M
N
O
P
Q
R
S
T
U
V
W
X
Y
Z

R

Rabbit on roller skates

S

Skunk on scooter

A B C D E F G H I J K L M N O P Q R S T U V W X Y Z

A
B
C
D
E
F
G
H
I
J
K
L
M
N
O
P
Q
R
S
T
U
V
W
X
Y
Z

T

Turtle at typewriter

U

Umpire under umbrella

A B C D E F G H I J K L M N O P Q R S T U V W X Y Z

A
B
C
D
E
F
G
H
I
J
K
L
M
N
O
P
Q
R
S
T
U
V
W
X
Y
Z

V

Vulture with violin

W

Walrus with wig

X

Xylophone for Xmas

A B C D E F G H I J K L M N O P Q R S T U V W X Y Z

Y

Yak with yo-yo

Z

Zebra with zither

P. D. Eastman

BIG DOG ...

LITTLE DOG

A Bedtime Story

Fred and Ted were friends.

Fred was big.

Ted was little.

Fred always had money.

Ted was always broke.

When they walked in the rain, Fred got wet but Ted stayed dry.

They both liked music.

Fred played the flute.
Ted played the tuba.

When they had dinner, Fred ate the spinach . . .
and Ted ate the beets.

When they painted the house,
Ted used red paint. Fred used green.

One day Fred and Ted took a trip.

Fred went in his green car.

Ted went in his red car.

Fred drove his car slowly.

Ted drove his car fast.

When they got to the mountains,
Ted skied all day long.

Fred skated all day long.

By nighttime both of them were very tired.
"Look!" said Fred. "A small hotel!"

Fred got a room upstairs.

Ted got a room downstairs.

"Good night, Ted.
Sleep well," said Fred.

"Good night, Fred.
Sleep well," said Ted.

But they did *not* sleep well. Upstairs, Fred thumped and bumped

And downstairs Ted moaned and groaned and crashed

nd tossed and turned.

nd thrashed all over the bed.

When morning came
Fred called on the phone.

"Let's take a walk,"
Fred said to Ted.

"A good idea!" said Ted to Fred.
"We can walk and talk."

They walked uphill.

They walked downhill.

They made tall talk.

They made small talk.

"Did you get any sleep last night, Ted?"

"Not a wink, Fred!"

"My bed is too little!"

"My bed is too big!"

"What can we
do about it, Ted?"
"I don't know, Fred."

"I know what to do!" said the bird.
"Just switch rooms. Ted should sleep upstairs
and Fred should sleep downstairs!"

"Of course!"

"The bird's
got the word."

"It's downstairs for me,"
yelled Fred.
    "It's upstairs for me,"
yelled Ted.

Ted jumped into the little bed upstairs.

And Fred jumped into the big bed downstairs.

Ted slept all day long in the cozy little bed.

And Fred slept all day in the cozy big bed.

"Well, that was easy to fix.
Big dogs need big beds.
Little dogs need little beds.

"Why make big problems
out of little problems?"